Olivia Lowery is a full-time elementary school educator of six years. In her first novel, *Captain Murphy and the Treasure of the Fifolet*, she explores her passion for adventure in a swashbuckling story based on her beloved Goldendoodle Murphy. She loves hiking and exploring her beautiful home state of Maine where she resides with her husband.

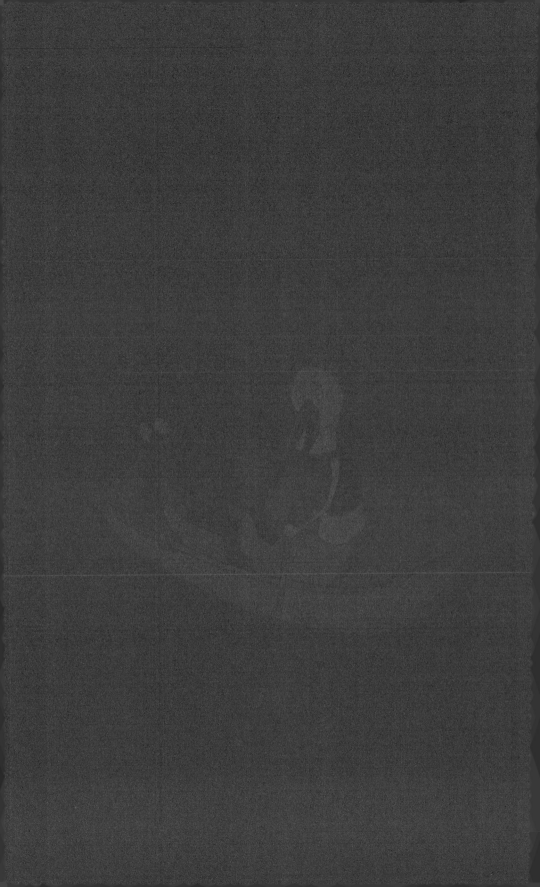

CAPTAIN
MURPHY AND THE
TREASURE
of the
FIFOLET

OLIVIA LOWERY

AUSTIN MACAULEY PUBLISHERS™
LONDON • CAMBRIDGE • NEW YORK • SHARJAH

Ordering Information
Quantity sales: Special discounts are available on quantity purchases by corporations, associations, and others. For details, contact the publisher at the address below.

Publisher's Cataloging-in-Publication data
Lowery, Olivia
Captain Murphy and the Treasure of the Fifolet

ISBN 9781649798251 (Paperback)
ISBN 9781649798268 (ePub e-book)

Library of Congress Control Number: 2022905246

www.austinmacauley.com/us

First Published 2023
Austin Macauley Publishers LLC
40 Wall Street, 33rd Floor, Suite 3302
New York, NY 10005
USA

mail-usa@austinmacauley.com
+1 (646) 5125767

To my Dad who taught me to dream and to my brothers who inspired this story.

For Murphy most of all.

Massive thanks to my wonderful husband and family who tirelessly supported me and read the awful first drafts. Thank you, Danny, for the characters and the tall tale. To my kiddos in the second grade, you inspire me to imagine and to remember the magic of childhood.

For my beautiful baby Murphy and the endless adventures and love.

Chapter One
New Orleans Docks 1929

Water splashed gently against the hulls of the boats, and the mist swirled around the two looming figures of the crocodiles that sauntered down the wharf in the dark, swinging their lanterns to the beat of the swinging jazz music that drifted down from the city and illuminating their toothy grins.

They stopped in front of a large wooden boat, shining the light on the name painted on the hull in bright red: Trouble II.

"This is it," the taller one growled to the other. They started up the gangplank. "Hold it right there, boys." They heard the low menacing growl from the shadows.

A surly bulldog stepped out into the lantern light.

"Captain," The first croc rumbled. "We're here to collect, the boss is getting impatient."

"Yeah," The other croc echoed. "Impatient." The captain narrowed his eyes.

"Just a little more time; he can give me just a little more time and he will get his money."

The crocs' eyes gleamed in the dark.

"Or we could just take your boat now."

"Come on, boys, just a few more days; I'll pay what I owe." The captain's voice had notes of desperation. "I can even give you something to tide you over, till I can scrounge something up. Here, take this." He pulled a shiny pocket watch from his jacket and dangled it in front of them.

The crocs' eyes widened. "Only a few days, then we're coming for the boat!" The tall one grabbed the watch and stuffed it in his pocket.

"Yeah, for the boat," the smaller one parroted back. They turned and disappeared into the dark, arguing over the watch.

The captain sighed and leaned against the railing. His whiskers were graying, and his eyes were drooping with a sad look from years of shrimping and troublesome times. He straightened the captain's cap on his ears and turned to duck into the hold of the boat.

Down in the hold, smoke filled the air, drifting from the pipe gripped in the beak of the gangly crane, captain's first mate, who was playing cards at a table with a young goggle-clad turtle.

"Provenzano send his thugs again?" the crane mumbled around the pipe.

"I bought us a few more days." The captain sighed as he sank into a chair, putting his paws on the table.

"How did you do that?" the turtle drawled.

"Distracted them with something shiny." The captain pulled out another shiny pocket watch from his jacket. "I keep a stash of cheap jewelry on hand for dumb reptiles."

He looked around "Where's Abelard?"

The portly possum bustled through the door as if on cue, carrying a rattling tray filled with beignets and hot coffee.

"I heard the crocs," he stuttered, "and so I made coffee."

The possum worked in the galley as the shrimp boat cook, and not only could he make the best jambalaya in the south but his response to any quandary was to fry up a batch of piping hot beignets and make coffee so black and strong that it could keep you on your toes for days.

They all helped themselves to sugary treats and steaming mugs. "Well I guess this is it," the crane mumbled.

"Unless any of you has a secret treasure buried somewhere."

They all leaned back in their chairs, letting the feeling that this was one of the last nights they would share as the crew of the shrimp boat fill the room, as thick and dreary as the pipe smoke.

Suddenly, the stillness of the night was shattered as the sound of angry shouts broke out on the wharf. There was a terrific clatter, and Abelard, the possum, scurried for the kitchen.

"What in tarnation?" The crane rearranged his gangly limbs to stand up quickly in annoyance, stalking up the steps to the deck.

"What's going on, Festus?" Captain called up the stairs.

"It's a lynch mob!" he called back. "From the riverboat! Looking for a fox!" He stalked back down the stairs.

"Some gambler made off with a small fortune." He sat back down and lit a pipe.

They had just gone back to their card game and Abelard had returned when they heard a scuffle on the deck above.

"Think it's the crocs again?" The turtle whispered as Abelard scuttled timidly back to the galley.

"We'll find out," said the captain, reaching for a crowbar that sat in the corner. The turtle gripped a large wrench and followed as they tiptoed up the stairs.

Festus watching from below with one talon on his vest, where he kept a small revolver.

The deck was dark and shadowy, the only light coming from the half-moon in the sky partially hidden by clouds and mist. They tiptoed around the deck.

"I don't see anything," The turtle whispered. They were about to go back down when a small scuffle came from inside an empty barrel.

He motioned to the turtle, and they tiptoed close to the barrel. Quickly, captain reached inside and pulled a fox from inside the barrel.

He gripped the fox by the collar of his tweed suit. The fox vigorously tried to escape, squirming and snarling with ferocity.

"Hey!" The turtle poked the fox. "You're the fellow they are looking for from that riverboat!"

The captain motioned, and the turtle tied the fox, avoiding the swinging paws.

They wrestled him into the hold.

"Unhand me, you river rats!" The fox shouted. "Let me go! Immediately!" "Hold him, Floyd!" the first mate barked to the turtle, who struggled to contain the writhing fox.

"Now see here," the captain growled sternly. "This is my boat. For now, at least, and I'd like to know what a sneaky fox is doing prowling around my deck in the wee hours!"

"That's got to be the gambler they were looking for from the riverboat that docked this morning, Captain." Festus assessed the fox. "We oughta turn him in, Captain."

Floyd poked the fox with his wrench, causing the fox to growl menacingly at the turtle, who backed away quickly.

"Let's not be hasty, gentlemen!" the fox pleaded. "Have a little heart!" He flashed a toothy grin.

"Nah, let's just turn him in, Captain," Festus mumbled, unaffected by the fox's charm, sitting back down to his cards.

"No good fox. Probably deserves a lynching."

"At least call the sheriff," Floyd chimed in, always one to be fair. The captain looked the fox up and down.

"Alright, Floyd, run into town and get the sheriff; let him know we got that fox everyone's looking for. He can decide what to do with you."

The fox squirmed in his ties. "No, no, not the law, please, I'll do anything, I'll-I'll-treasure!" he shouted. "I can bring you to a treasure." The captain turned to look at him.

"What treasure?"

The fox, sensing he had caught the attention of the crew, quickly responded, eyes gleaming.

"Jean Lafitte, the pirate. I know where he buried a treasure. I learned from a man whose grandfather sailed with him. I can take you right to it. I have a map!"

Festus stood up from the table.

"He's lying, Captain. No one knows where the treasure is, no one living. He'll say anything to save his skin."

The fox cried out, "No, no! I swear it's true. Check my pockets! The map is there!"

Festus looked at the captain, who nodded, and checked the pockets of the tweed suit. He found a crumpled, yellowed piece of paper scrawled with lines and symbols.

"I won it," the fox said. "Well, perhaps 'acquired' it is a better word," he amended as the captain raised a shaggy eyebrow.

"It can't be real; no one living knows where the treasure was hidden. It's all fable," Festus said after examining it.

The captain took the map from him and scanned it with a peculiar expression on his face.

"Maybe this is it," he muttered. "Maybe it's our chance."

He looked up at his crew. "It's worth a shot, after all. We are going to lose the boat anyway if we don't. What harm could there be in trying?"

"Really?" Floyd queried.

"You aren't serious," Festus said with a look of disbelief. "This is crazy! We can't find that treasure. The map probably isn't even real."

"Oh, but it is!" the fox spouted off. "It is very real; the man I acquired it from saw it with his own eyes."

The captain looked at Festus. Festus threw up a talon.

"No! No, no, no, no! Don't think that you can just look at me with those puppy eyes and I will just agree to this. This is craziness! There is no way I am going to go with you into the bayou on some ridiculous treasure hunt."

Floyd looked between the two, back and forth, back and forth as the captain held Festus's gaze. After a brief pause, Festus let out an enormous sigh.

"Alriiight!" He shook a talon at the captain. "But I still think it's a stupid idea."

The next morning at dawn, the crew got the boat ready to set out. The fox remained tied up in the hold on the condition that he would be released once they had left the city. The captain agreed to hide the fox on the boat until they made it to the treasure; they would split the treasure and go their separate ways.

As the boat drew in the anchor and set off, chugging quietly into the bay, Brutus and Nero, the crocodile henchmen, watched from the wharf.

They returned to the quarter, letting themselves into a large building with a courtyard. They stood by the fountain and waited. On the balcony a vulture appeared, large and imposing in a silk top hat, a monocle magnifying one eye to glare at them from above.

"They left, boss," Brutus, the larger one, said in a subservient tone. "They pulled anchor at dawn and left."

"Yeah, boss," the younger croc, Nero, repeated. "They left." The vulture let out an irritated squawk.

"Where did they go?" he demanded.

"Uh, I don't know, boss," Brutus mumbled. "What?" the vulture glared.

"He said we don't know, boss," Nero echoed.

"I heard him!" screeched the vulture, "You let them go!"

"Uh-uh-sorry, boss," muttered the croc, shifting from side to side nervously. "Well, don't just stand there!" The vulture flapped his wings. "Follow them!"

His screech reverberated through the courtyard as the crocs hurried out into the street, toward the wharf, where they slipped below the water and disappeared all but for their beady eyes moving silently across the surface, following the boat as it headed out into the murky darkness.

Chapter Two

In another part of town, a darkly-clad martin slipped through the streets and, knocking at the door, he was met by a maid and entered a tall, beautiful townhouse.

The maid led him through ornate hallways and into a study lit by flickering firelight.

Inside, a tall, handsome martin was on the floor playing a game with his three tiny fur-ball children. Their delighted squeaks caused the mother, who watched from a lounge chair by the fireplace, to smile softly.

The maid announced his presence. "Giacomo here to see you, Mr. Sylvester."

Sylvester stood up from the floor, brushing the dust from his jacket and shooed the children out the door.

"Goodnight, children." He tapped each furry head as it went by. He lightly kissed their mother as she followed them. "Goodnight, dear."

Giacomo closed the door after them, and the two took armchairs by the fire. "The vulture?" Sylvester inquired.

The martin opposite him was quiet and sleek, dressed neatly in a pressed gray suit.

"The vulture is refusing to shut down his operations," Giacomo quietly responded.

Sylvester put his chin in his paw and frowned. "We are not going to let this slide."

He appeared to think for a moment.

"Take some men. Go to his house, send him a message. No one messes with this family."

Giacomo nodded. "Yes, boss." Then he left.

Sylvester remained for a while, leaned back in the armchair, the firelight flickering across his stony face.

On board the shrimp boat, the captain stood at the wheel, squinting into the rising sun as he steered the boat through the water. Festus came to stand behind him.

"We've got the fox changed into something a little less conspicuous."

"He still tied up?" asked the captain.

"For now," Festus replied, leaning against the rail. "At least until we are a little farther from shore."

The bayou was beautiful; water lilies swarmed with dragonflies, buzzing and dancing on the humid morning air. The sun was filtering through the trees overhead and the birds sang cheerily.

That day, they carefully meandered through the swamp, making their way through the shallows, avoiding sandbars.

The fox finally came up from the hold, released by a reluctant Festus. He looked out of place in the grease-stained and tattered trousers, and suspenders that Floyd had shared from his own gear. They hung off of him in an entirely different way than the tailored tweed suit, and his ruffled fur no longer resembled the sleek fox of the night before.

The captain nodded at the fox. "Morning," he grunted.

The fox held out a slender paw. "Clovis, Clovis the fox at your service."

The captain took the paw and shook it. "Captain, just Captain, at yours."

The water was shallow, and as the sun went down it became almost impossible to see what was ahead, even in the lantern light. They chugged slowly along, taking great care.

Festus, Floyd, and Abelard were below deck with Clovis, enticed by Abelard's hot coffee. The captain stayed at the wheel, bantering with Marcel, the incredibly old river rat.

He was wrinkled, tired, old and extremely useless as a crewmember, but he stayed aboard for nostalgia's sake, occasionally offering up some little bit of wisdom that they always ignored, and always wished they hadn't.

The crunch was unmistakable as the boat lurched. They had hit something.

Festus and Floyd rushed up from below deck. "What happened? What did we hit?"

Floyd had his tool box in hand. He hopped overboard and waded through the shallow water.

"It's a log!" he called up. "Caught on the rudder, knocked a piece right off! We're gonna need to stop and fix it."

Grumbling, the captain and Festus set to work, dropping anchor and making ready to stop for the night.

The boat bustled as Floyd set to work on the rudder, fixing it with the speed of a skilled craftsman. Abelard went to work on a crawfish boil, and soon the night air was full of the perfume of spicy Cajun cooking and delicious hot coffee. The lantern lights from the boat gleamed and reflected off of the water.

They all sat down and enjoyed the meal while Marcel played a soulful melody on the saxophone, the sound mixing with the crickets, frogs, and cicadas in a magnificent night orchestra.

No one noticed the beady eyes watching them from afar as the crocs lay submerged in the shadows, sliding through the water.

Festus lit a pipe, tipping his chair back and blowing a perfect smoke ring into the night. Clovis regaled them with stories of places he had seen on the riverboat and people he had met, such as an old, rich otter with an impressive mustache who had an unfortunate tendency to spend his money at the tables and lose great amounts of it to none other than Clovis, a sly little minx that hopped from boat to boat picking pockets and selling the things he collected, and a beautiful snake that beguiled rich boat patrons with her large hypnotic eyes.

Festus remarked that all Clovis's acquaintances were as shady as he.

Captain spread the map out on the table, marking where they were in correspondence to the X.

"About another day and we should be close to the treasure." Marcel put down the saxophone and narrowed his eyes at the crew. "Treasure?"

"The treasure of Jean Lafitte!" Floyd confirmed.

"The treasure of the Fifolet," Marcel corrected firmly, shaking his head.

"A dead man's dream." Marcel frowned before picking up the saxophone and playing a mournful tune.

The captain waved his paw to dismiss the warning words. "So what exactly is this Fifolet of great legend?" Floyd asked.

Marcel's eyes gleamed as he relished the opportunity to tell a story.

"Back in the glory days of the pirates, when my grandfather was a boy, there was a pirate whose ferocity and ruthlessness surpassed all of the others: Jean Lafitte! He had the fastest ship and the bravest crew. As the legend goes, Jean Lafitte buried his vast treasure in the bayou. To protect it, he killed the cruelest member of his crew and buried him with it, with the intention that the ghost will guard the treasure for all eternity. To this day, the blue lighted Fifolet roams the bayou, luring travelers to the treasure, and the travelers…" He paused for effect. "Are never seen again!"

Festus rolled his eyes.

"And if you believe a word that old rat says, you are crazier than he is." He shoved Floyd jovially, and they all laughed.

Hidden beneath the shadow of the overhanging trees, the two crocs exchanged grins, having heard every word. And by the time the sun rose, a swift-winged bird was on its way back to the quarter bearing the message from the vulture's henchmen. The captain was on a treasure hunt, and no one went without paying dues to the vulture.

Chapter Three

The next day, with the rudder fixed, they set off again deeper into the swamp.

The crew lounged on deck in the humid sunlight, excitement brimming. Festus looked up from the map he had spread over a crate.

"This is Marie's neck of the woods, Captain; best to pay our respects." Clovis looked between them. "Who is Marie?" he asked.

"A witch; she lives in the swamp nearby. Hearsay has it, she practices very powerful voodoo. She is very well respected."

The captain responded, "This is her territory. And it's always best to be very respectful to someone like Marie."

Clovis sat back, eyes wide.

The crew became very quiet as the canal narrowed, and the water darkened. The birds were silent, and there was a mysterious air about the swamp. It began to rain softly as the skies darkened, and the water lapped angrily at the boat.

"This is some kinda something you'd read in a book," Floyd muttered, his forehead creased with worry.

"Look!" Clovis pointed anxiously at the trees.

Hanging from the limbs were charms and sparkling objects. Abelard's frantic movements were heard below deck, loudly clattering pots and pans, as if he could sense the unease of the crew above.

As they turned a corner, a shack came into view, stilted above the swamp and hidden slightly behind tall trees. It loomed ominously in front of them. An iron fence, decora.tive and threatening, made a jagged line across the front of the house, standing on the bits of firm ground scattered in the muck.

The gate creaked on its hinges, swaying gently in the wind. The captain looked sideways at Festus, who was clutching his hat in his talons and nervously puffing on his cigar, billowing the fragrant smoke around his head like a cloud.

"Golly!" exclaimed Marcel. "It's been years and years since I've seen Miss Marie."

The captain nodded, his face frozen in an expression that had Clovis looking back and forth between the crew members.

"What, may I ask, is the matter with the captain?" Clovis enquired quietly to Floyd. "One would think he had seen a ghost."

Floyd whispered, "Miss Marie and the Captain used to be close, you could say." He raised his eyebrows knowingly.

"You mean?" Clovis stuttered. Floyd nodded smugly.

The captain and Marcel set off down the gangplank, slowly making their way along the patches of grass, through the gate and up to the steps of the shack. Marcel looked back and winked, flicking his tattered tail before following the captain to the door. Before they could knock, the door opened.

"Meeercy," said Floyd, "I got the shivers. Coffee, anyone?" He elbowed Clovis. "Come below deck and I'll tell you all about the Cap and Miss Marie."

They all agreed and scurried below deck to the security of Abelard's cooking.

Inside the shack, the lighting was dim, coming from what seemed like hundreds of candles scattered all over the expanse of the interior. Bundles of herbs hung from the rafters, and dozens of bottles cluttered the shelves on the wall.

The table in the center of the room was covered in papers, yellowed and tattered, and books were stacked on one another into a tower that leaned precariously.

"Well, gentlemen," a coy voice from behind them spoke. "What brings you to my part of the bayou?"

They turned swiftly, and there in the candlelight stood the most beautiful black cat, sleek and shining in the light. The captain's breath caught.

"Well, hasn't it just been forever," she purred, circling the captain and Marcel, her gleaming teeth snapping at the rat's tail as she passed.

Marcel squeaked and leaped into the captain's pocket.

"You couldn't possibly be here just to visit little old me, could you now, boo?" She ran her tail over the captain's shoulders, flicking the cap off his head.

"On our way, passing through," the captain growled in a low tone. "Just paying our respects, Marie."

She leaned back on the table.

"Well now," she purred "Isn't that just sweeeeet." The captain stood his ground.

"You haven't changed a bit." His tone was softer. "As enchanting as ever."

"Well, you have," she snapped. "You look old now, Murphy." Her eyes narrowed into glowing slits. "Don't think I've forgotten what you did back then." Her voice took on a hurt note. "And don't you think I've forgiven." She turned her back, her tail flicking in annoyance.

"I'm sorry, Marie." The captain shrugged.

"Oh well." She turned to face him, a huge mischievous smile replacing the look of hurt on her face, her ears pricked. "Bygones, darling. How can I help you?"

The captain shifted his weight uncomfortably. "We are in a bit of a bind. The vulture."

"I suppose he wants the boat?" she surmised. "Well, that's your trouble to bear, beb, not mine. But what then brings you to the bayou? You don't think you can run from the vulture, do you? Provenzano always gets what he wants. You should never have gotten involved with the families."

"You know I had no choice," the captain said sadly. "He was the only one with enough money to help me."

Marie was silent, but the tension and sadness between them was palpable.

"And in the end it couldn't save her," the captain said, his voice cracking. "So, no. I don't think I can run." The captain shook his head. "We are, well, on a bit of a hunt."

"A hunt?" She tilted her head inquisitively.

"Treasure," the captain said, and with that one word, Marie's eyes blazed.

"Jean Lafitte?" she exclaimed. "The Fifolet! Murphy, you don't realize what you are up against. That kind of magic should not be disturbed."

The captain rolled his eyes. "Marie, the Fifolet? That's just a legend." The cat's voice grew low and menacing.

"Don't be so quick to discredit legends. That was always your mistake; you have no belief."

She rustled through clutter on the shelves, looking for something before turning back to the captain.

"They say the devil himself guards the treasure, Murphy. No one has ever survived when they meet the fifolet. Please, don't do this foolish thing."

The captain reached up and smoothed the fur behind the cat's silky ears. "Well, I've never turned down a foolish thing, Marie," he mumbled.

"I knew you would say that, you old fool," she said ruefully. "Here, Murphy." She held out a charm on a long silver chain. "This could protect you from the Devil himself."

She slipped it over his head and under his jacket. "Come back to me this time," she murmured.

Then, in a whirl, a force shoved him out the door and the candlelight was gone, eliminated in a second. He turned to the shack, and it was as dark as midnight. Empty.

They reached the boat, and he paused on deck before joining the crew in the galley, looking back at the shack. He sighed tremendously and touched the charm around his neck.

"Well," squeaked Marcel from his pocket. "She seemed happy to see you."

The captain swatted his pocket, but the rat was already scuttling along the deck, laughing before disappearing into a hole in the cabin.

The captain stood for a while, staring into the night, thinking. He was completely lost in thought, unaware that Festus had joined him on deck and stood next to him.

"So, Marie?"

The captain nodded. "Got an extra cigar?" Festus smiled. "That bad, huh?"

He pulled a cigar from his pocket, cut it, and lit it before handing it to the captain.

The captain nodded his thanks and puffed the cigar gratefully.

They stood there for a while, the only sound made by the crickets and the soft rain. The smoke mixed with the scent of the bayou, familiar to both of them, taking them back to a time when they were younger.

Chapter Four

That night, they were awakened by piercing howls and scuffling. The whole crew piled out of bed and scrambled for their clothes and weapons. Marcel's squeals were heard above, and with a growl, the captain grabbed the sawed-off shotgun from the corner, pulled on his boots, and stormed up the stairs. Festus followed, armed to the beak with knives and razor-sharp talons.

At the top of the stairs, they were greeted by the sight of a mangy coyote pack spread out on the deck, the one in the front dangling Marcel from a claw and grinning a toothy grin.

"Well, Captain," the leader spoke with slick contempt. "Fancy seeing you here." The captain planted his paws on the deck and growled.

"Let him go, Rex."

The leader of the coyotes laughed, the sound echoing in the night. "That's a big bark, Captain. If only your bite lived up to it."

The captain snarled, and Festus tightened his talon around a long bowie knife in his belt.

"We don't want any trouble, Captain." Rex had a smooth, silky voice that was deceptively disarming. "We are looking for a fox, fancy man, a gambler from one of the riverboats. There's quite a bounty on him. Seen anything suspicious?"

As he spoke, he flung Marcel onto the deck with a twitch of his paw. Marcel scurried away and disappeared into the shadows, squeaking his dismay.

"Haven't seen a thing," the captain spoke in a guarded tone.

"Is that so?" Rex drawled, moving closer, flanked by the pack of leering bounty hunters. "Because word has it all over this bayou that you and your crew have a fox aboard."

He snapped the last words, teeth clashing together, shining in the moonlight. The captain bared his teeth. "I said, haven't seen a thing."

Clovis picked that inopportune moment to step from lower deck, a small revolver tucked in his slender paw.

"Well, well, well," chuckled the coyote. "Is that a fox I see?" He flexed his claws. "We'll just take him off your hands now, Captain."

As they stepped forward, the captain leveled the shotgun on Rex and growled. "Not another step."

Clovis cocked the revolver and braced himself; Festus drew the knife and stepped into a fighting stance.

"So this is the way it's gonna be, then?" Rex growled. "After all we've been through." He clicked.

"Guess so." The captain's eyes glinted a silent dare to the pack.

"Looks like only three of you to me," the coyote growled. "You sure you want to do this? Wouldn't it be simpler to just hand him over now?"

"Four," piped up Floyd from the stairs as he stepped onto the deck, holding a giant wrench in each hand.

"Five." Abelard's shaky voice came from behind the tommy gun he held in his suddenly rock-steady paws. The rest of the crew stepped aside, allowing him to move to the front, the captain on his left.

Rex snarled as he took in the situation. Coyotes hunted in packs, preying on the weak, the sick, and the defenseless. Suddenly, the crew wasn't looking weak or defenseless. Staring straight into the barrel of a tommy gun will take the

courage out of the bravest animal.

He backed away with the pack, down the gangplank, growling as he went.

"This isn't over, Captain. We'll be back, and the next time you won't be so lucky."

As the coyotes retreated into the night, the crew breathed a collaborative sigh of relief. Clovis was staring at Abelard, mouth gaping.

"I thought he-aren't you…? But… Pardon my language, but I took you for a fraidy well, possum. Shouldn't you be playing dead right now?!"

Festus laughed. "Sometimes it's the people you least expect."

Floyd shook his finger at the possum. "I knew you didn't really play the violin!" Abelard only blushed as he whisked the gun back to its case in the kitchen, straightening his apron.

Chapter Five

Back in the quarter, the murky darkness of the street was pierced by the dim lights coming from the St. Charles tavern. Owned by the reigning gangster family, it was closed at the late hour, but inside, sitting at one of the tables, sat the Old Father himself.

The Old Father reclined against the back of his chair, his face creased and lined with age and many years of worry. His fur was thin and patchy, but he wore his suit neatly. At his side sat Sylvester. His demeanor was sharp and cold, and his eyes were steely and black as they stared at the door, waiting. His whiskey swirled gently in the glass he held. They were flanked by a fat old martin who had seen better days but held his sawed-off shotgun with authority that spoke of years filled with trouble.

Glasses clinked quietly behind them at the bar. A young martin, Sylvester's cousin, moved gracefully as she wiped down the bar and polished the glasses. Her hips swished, and her eyes snapped with excitement. She was the only woman in the family who was involved in the affairs directly; her heart of iron and her devious charm combined with a striking beauty made her an invaluable asset. Not to mention her skill with the revolver she kept tucked beneath her skirt.

There was a flurry of motion outside, then the door opened, slamming against the wall as Giacomo entered, holding a trembling weasel in front of him, a revolver against his spine. The music that had filtered in when they opened the door ended abruptly as it was slammed closed. Giacomo shoved the weasel to the floor, cowering and disheveled.

"Here he is, boss." Giacomo stepped back, the barrel of his gun still trained on the weasel.

"Alfonso." Sylvester sighed, his calm demeanor giving no sign as to his seething anger. "What have you done?"

Giacomo glared at the cowering figure, grief in his face. The weasel made to stand, but the sound of Salvatore shucking shells into the chamber sent him back to his knees.

"Please, Sir," he whimpered. "Please, I had no choice. They threatened me!" The weasel wrung his thin paws.

"You do not trust me to protect you? You coward!" Sylvester hissed. "Because of you and your disloyalty, my men were killed. Good men, men with families. Men who trusted you to lead them, not to betray them to Provenzano. My godchildren are now without a father."

One of the fat guards bared his teeth. "It was a bloodbath, Alfonso." He held up his bandaged leg. "I was the only one who made it out. The only one except you. How much did the vulture pay you? The boys who died were my friends." His teeth snapped together as he spat the words out, causing the weasel to wince.

The Old Father remained silent, although he missed nothing, his eyes glinting over the whole scene. Sylvester looked to him now as a sign of respect, requesting a blessing on his verdict. The Old Father knew what the look meant and nodded his approval. Sylvester turned to face the weasel.

"Alfonso, you have betrayed the family. Your disloyalty and your cowardice cannot be forgiven. I am afraid you are no longer a friend to us."

He motioned with a hand for a guard. The old, fat martin moved forward, wheezing he grabbed the weasel by an arm, and together he and Giacomo lifted the creature.

"Take him away." Sylvester waved a hand. "Send him to purgatory."

The weasel begged for mercy as he was led out the back door. Elena refilled their drinks. They were silent.

After a while, Giacomo returned.

"Salvatore is taking care of it," he said quietly. Sylvester stood.

"I think it is time we deal with Provenzano for once and for all," he said firmly. "I need you to gather the men. We are going to pay the vulture a visit."

Elena's eyes blazed.

"The vulture has just left for the bayou." She tossed her hair. "His scaly thugs have a treasure for him."

Sylvester raised a brow and stroked his whiskers. "Then let's take this battle to the bayou."

The Old Father, Matranga, laid a wrinkled paw on Sylvester's arm. "Watch for the coyotes," he quavered. "And pay your respects to Marie." Sylvester nodded in obedience.

"Elena, stay with my wife and the children. If anything happens, protect them."

Nodding, she wrapped her coat around her shoulders and headed into the dark, leaving the two fathers, old and new, to rule their city from the tavern, whiskey in hand, awaiting the sunrise and the trouble to come.

Chapter Six

On the shrimp boat, they floated uneventfully all the next day, and by the time the sun set, they were deep in the swamp. The night was peaceful, almost magical, and the fireflies lit up the swamp, dancing over the water to the music of Marcel's saxophone. The crew was lounging on deck, mid-match in a game of cards, when Festus straightened, staring off into the distance.

"Did you see that?" he questioned Floyd. "The light!"

Floyd poked the crane's wing, ruffling his feathers. "Festus is seeing the light, fellows; looks like it's all over for this guy."

Festus rearranged his feathers disgruntledly and stretched out a talon to point at the trees. "Look, don't you see it? The light."

"The captain followed his gaze, and as the crew turned to look, they froze. There was a light. A shining blue orb floated gracefully in the air amid the trees.

The blue glow lit up a path, winding into the darkness. Marcel dropped the saxophone, letting it fall to the deck with a clatter.

"The Fifolet!" he croaked.

The captain examined the map. "This is it!"

Festus stuttered. "You mean we are going to follow that thing? To the treasure?" The captain nodded grimly.

"If Marcel is to be believed, the legend says that the light of the Fifolet roams the forest near the treasure."

The captain began barking orders to set anchor, ready for landing, and bring shovels.

"Oh sure, listen to that part of the story," Marcel chirped.

The crew scurried to obey orders, and Marcel squeaked from his trembling perch on the rail.

"Beware the Fifolet, Captain. Beware the ghost light." The captain simply rolled his eyes and joined the crew.

"I think I will be better off waiting here," Clovis interjected as the crew began to set off down the gangplank.

"What?" shouted Festus, whirling to the fox. "You coward!" he squawked, his beak alarmingly close to the fox's face.

Clovis cringed backward.

"It's just that, you wanted me to lend you my map, and that I have done," he spluttered.

Festus glowered at the fox, who backed slowly away.

"I've never been one with a shovel, and I am sure I will only slow you down," Clovis croaked.

"Just leave him," The captain growled. His tone showed the disappointment he felt.

"Should have known you were just as selfish as ever," Festus spat.

"I thought you were different," Floyd said sadly as he passed the fox. Always one for fairness and kindness, he had begun to take a liking to the fox.

"We've no idea what we are walking into here," The captain said. "Best we don't have anyone along who would stab us in the back anyways." He turned and walked down the gangplank.

The crew followed the captain down the gangplank, leaving Clovis standing alone and sheepish on the deck.

The crew, armed with shovels, picks, and axes, set off into the black night of the forest, lanterns swinging. The blue orb of light floated in front of them, always out of reach, yet close enough to see, to lead them on through the trees.

Festus grumbled around his cigar as they walked. "Crazy shenanigans. Ought not bother the dead. Fool's errand. Probably no treasure anyway."

The captain shot a glare his way, silencing him.

Waiting until the crew were out of earshot, the crocs slithered out of the murky water. They watched as the crew disappeared into the forest, unwilling to follow the orb or the crew to what they deemed certain death.

Unaware of Clovis's presence, there they would have stayed, had the silence of the night not been broken by the furious flapping of wings and the screech they knew all too well. Clovis ducked behind a barrel at the sound, listening from the shadows as the vulture landed.

The vulture landed atop Brutus and glared furiously at the pair.

"How dare you disrespect me in this way?" he screeched, driving his beak into Brutus's scaly head. "I said follow them! And here you are!"

"But boss," Nero croaked. "The Fifolet, we saw it; it leads them to the treasure."

The vulture's eyes gleamed. "So the stories are true, then. The treasure is real." His greed was almost palpable, and the crocs squirmed.

"I suppose I will have to find henchmen more loyal to their boss, more eager to serve, men with half an ounce of courage," the vulture screamed at the crocs. "Luckily, I planned ahead."

The crocs jumped as the shadowy forms of the coyote pack emerged in front of them, Rex in the lead, leering at the crocs with a sinister stare.

The vulture ordered the pack into the forest, and they leaped away on the trail of the crew, quickly disappearing into the dark. The vulture gave one last angry squawk at the crocs. "I'll deal with you later," he said venomously before flapping his wings loudly and following the coyotes.

The crocs exchanged looks.

"Don't you got a cousin down in the gulf?" Brutus asked.

Nero nodded, and the two slipped into the water, swimming for Texas with surprising speed.

Clovis ducked out from behind the barrel when the coast was clear. "No!" he whispered.

He rubbed his ears with his paws anxiously.

"What are you going to do?" squeaked Marcel from his perch on the roof of the boat.

"Yipes!" Yelped Clovis, startled.

He leaped into the air as Marcel cackled.

"What are you doing here?" Clovis asked, his tone accusing.

"Somebody had to stay and guard the boat from selfish foxy boy," The rat taunted.

"Yeah." Clovis whooshed out a breath. "What can we do?" he asked the rat.

"The captain isn't going to have any idea that they're on his tail! The coyotes are going to ambush them!"

"Yep," Marcel said.

He leapt off of the roof and perched on Clovis's shoulder. "Unless somebody warns them," he squeaked.

"You mean?" Clovis asked, gesturing to himself.

"Who else?" the rat exclaimed. "I'm too old to make it there in time!" Clovis growled.

"Oh, FINE!" he said, stamping his paw on the deck. "You're right."

Marcel cackled from his perch and hopped into the front pocket of Clovis's shirt. "Let's go, foxy boy!" he screeched.

Clovis took off, bounding through the darkness.

"You know I've always been afraid of ghosts!" he whined.

"You're in for all kinds of trouble then." Marcel laughed.

Chapter Seven

The light danced around them, following them through the forest in what seemed like circles.

They followed the captain as he carefully followed the map. His snout pressed close to it. Festus held a lantern so that the captain could read the map and see ahead of them as they stepped carefully through the woods. The path was tricky. They proceeded cautiously, avoiding patches of mud that could swallow them whole.

"Does this whole thing seem just a bit too easy?" Festus asked warily. "Yeah," Floyd echoed.

"From all the legends," Festus continued, "Jean Lafitte was an old rascal. I'd tread lightly, captain."

"Oh, don't you worry about me," The captain said easily. "I know how to follow a map—ahhhh!" he shouted as the path seemed to dissolve beneath him and he disappeared.

"Captain!" the crew cried in unison.

They lurched forward, careful to avoid the gaping hole where the captain had been standing.

"Captain?" they asked, peering down into the dark abyss below. There was no sign of him.

Suddenly a whimper pierced the air. "SNAKES!" Captain yelped from inside the hole. "Snakes?" Festus called down.

"What's going on, Captain?" Floyd called down after.

"GET ME OUT OF HERE! THERE ARE SNAKES!" the Captain screamed. "Yes, sir!" Festus yelled.

They scrambled for the rope that they had slung into one of the packs.

Floyd tossed the rope down into the hole and wrapped the other end around his stout shell.

Before they could blink, the captain came scrambling up the rope.

He was shaking, and his tail was tucked so far between his legs it was nearly invisible.

"Um, Captain-" Festus pointed at the captain.

"You, uh…you have something right there," Floyd stuttered.

He pointed to a large snake that clung to the captain's hat. The snake curled around the brim and hissed.

The captain whirled desperately, trying to see what had escaped the hole with him.

"Where?!" he whined like a puppy. "Get it off! Get it off of me!" he yelped.

Festus flapped his wings and squawked loudly. Floyd backed away, his eyes wide. "Snakes are not my thing!" Floyd shook his head.

"Someone do something!" Captain wailed.

"I've got it!" shouted Abelard, barreling out of the woods with a large stick.

He swung the stick over his head and used it to whack the captain's hat. The hat flew off of his head and sailed into the underbrush, the snake still along for the ride.

The captain stopped spinning and dropped to the ground, panting. His eyes were wide and his hackles were raised. The crew was silent for a moment; then they erupted in laughter. The captain snarled softly under his breath, annoyed.

He scrambled onto his hind paws and brushed off his seat. "We'd best keep going." He glowered at the crew.

"This time…" Festus shook the tip of his wing at the captain, "…you'd better watch where you are going."

Captain shook his head and started down through the woods again, following the map closely. The path was dark and hard to see. Captain took the lead, holding a lantern high.

The Fifolet wove through the trees, back and forth ahead of them. "It seems like it is trying to lead us off the path!" Festus said warily.

"It keeps circling back like it wants us to follow it," Floyd said, agreeing with Festus.

"Don't follow it!" Captain said firmly. "Marcel says that the light lures folk off of the trail and to their death."

"Yeesh." Floyd grimaced. "That sounds unpleasant."

"Its job is to protect the treasure." Festus shrugged. "That does make sense."

"We follow the map and we watch our step," Captain said. He stopped then, causing Festus to bump into him. "Hey!" Festus chirped.

"What's going on?" Floyd poked his head around Festus to look at the captain.

"The map doesn't make any sense." The captain scratched his ears. "Why not?" Festus said, peering at the map over the captain's shoulder.

"It looks like there should be a huge rock right here," Captain said, puzzled. "We must be lost," Festus groaned. "We should try to find that rock. It must be close; we've been following all the right clues."

"This can't be right," the captain said, staring at the map thoughtfully.

"Let's see if it is up ahead," Floyd said. "Maybe we just haven't gone far enough. He stepped around the captain to keep going.

"Wait," said the captain, but Floyd continued on. "This seems kind of… odd," Abelard mused, frowning.

Captain looked up from the map in time to see Floyd, about to step directly onto a pile of leaves.

"Watch out!" Captain yelled.

He dropped the map and dove toward Floyd, tackling him as he stepped onto the leaves.

The leaves brushed aside, and they heard a faint CLICK.

The captain grabbed Floyd around his shell and rolled to the side as quickly as he could. Just in time, as a boulder came crashing down from the treetops above. The boulder landed with a gargantuan crash in the exact place that Floyd had been standing.

Floyd poked his head out from under the captain and grunted. "You're crushing me," he gasped.

"So much for a thank you," Captain huffed, rolling off of the turtle.

"And besides," Festus gaped. "That rock would've crushed your shell for real." He motioned with his wings. "SPLAT!"

Floyd took the captain's outstretched hand and stood up. His legs trembled as stood and stared at the boulder that now sat on the forest floor.

"You must have stepped on a pressure plate," Captain said, leaning down to inspect the base of the boulder, which was now resting where a plate may have been. Floyd just stood there, continuing to stare.

"Well," he said finally. His eyes were huge with shock. "At least we know that we are in the right place now."

"It appears that we are," Captain agreed wryly.

"This is it then," Festus said, appraising the rock. "What's next? Fire?" he joked. Captain made a face, and Festus shook his head.

"You've got to be kidding me!" Abelard squeaked anxiously.

Captain nodded. He looked up and down from the map. He sighed, and his eyes were wide. "The next clue does indeed look like--"

"Don't say it." Festus buried his beak in his wing. "Fire."

They nearly tiptoed as they carefully kept moving through the woods. The captain's ears were pricked. They were all on their toes, waiting for the next surprise.

The woods echoed with the sounds of wind in the treetops and the eerie noise of the coyotes in the distance.

"That light is giving me the heebie jeebies!" Floyd shivered in his shell, tucking his neck further into the sanctuary of it.

"Try to ignore it," the captain said quietly.

"Uh, Captain," Abelard said, his voice shaky. He pointed to one of the trees. "That doesn't look too good to me," he squeaked.

They looked at the tree and gasped as one. The tree, and many of the others around them, were covered in deep gashes.

"Claws!" gulped Floyd.

"A m-m-monster!" Abelard trembled. Even Festus seemed afraid.

"Now, don't you worry," the captain said. "We made it this far. We can keep going. Think of the treasure, boys."

He tried to sound convincing, but the crew knew him well enough to see the fear in his eyes.

They kept going, rounding a massive tree. Suddenly, the sound of angry squawking filled the air as Festus was swept up into the trees. He flapped his wings against the net that held him, but he could not get free. He screeched and pecked at the net with his beak.

"Festus!" the crew yelled.

They looked around frantically for the tripwire that had activated the trap. As they did so, Floyd stumbled over a fallen log and fell to the ground. He landed on his back, his legs flailing in the air.

As he rolled on his shell, trying desperately to get to his feet, he rolled over a lever. He heard the loud CLICK once again.

"No no no no no!" he shouted, rolling as hard as he could.

This time, nothing fell from the sky. Instead, all around where they stood, a blaze erupted. The pressure plate had sparked a flame that burst up along the lines of oil that ringed the trees. They were surrounded with a wall of fire. Festus began to screech louder from his trap, high above in the trees.

"Beeeeeeeeeees!" he screamed.

"Please?" Captain yelled up. "No need to beg, we are looking for a way to get you down."

"No beeeeees!" Festus shouted. "There are bees up here!"

"Listen, Festus," Floyd shouted up. "We are trying our best, no need to beg!"

Festus screeched even louder. This time the whole crew heard as he screamed at the top of his lungs.

"GET ME DOWN, THERE ARE BEEEEEEEEEEEES UP HERE!"

"Oh! Bees!" Captain said. "Gotcha." "What do we do?" Floyd shouted. "Fire!" Abelard shouted.

"We know there's a fire," Floyd said impatiently, turning to the possum. "We are trying to save Festus from the bees right now, Abelard."

"No, no," Captain said, "Abelard is on to something. We need to smoke out the bees."

"Ohhhh." Floyd nodded, understanding.

Abelard snatched up a stick from the forest floor. He ripped part of his shirt and wrapped it around the stick. He dipped it into the flames, and it lit up.

"Here!" Captain said, taking the torch from Abelard. "Climb up the tree and smoke them out!"

Abelard scrambled up the tree, clinging to the bark with his claws. When he was nearly to where Festus hung from the branches, he stopped.

"There's definitely bees up here!" Abelard squealed. "And OH BOY are they mad!"

He held out a paw, and Cap threw the torch with all of his might. Abelard strained, reaching out to catch it with one paw. The torch sailed through the air. Abelard leaned out as far as he could, stretching his paw. He caught the torch and held it high, holding the smoke underneath the beehive.

Slowly, the bees began to dissipate, calmed by the smoke. When the last of the bees were gone, he dropped the torch to where the captain waited below. Captain caught the torch, and Abelard scooted up the tree to Festus. Festus was curled up into a ball of feathers inside the net. His wings were flared to protect him from the sting of the bees.

Abelard set to work, chewing on the ropes. He paused in his work long enough to yell out to Festus.

"Better spread those wings, buddy!"

"What?" Festus said, poking his head out from beneath his wings.

Just then, Abelard chewed through the last of the ropes, and the net let loose.

Festus let out a loud noise as he plummeted to the ground. At last, he spread his wings and caught himself before he hit the ground.

He flapped his wings angrily and settled back to the ground as Abelard slid down the tree to join the rest of the crew.

"Wheeeeeeee-youuuuu!" Abelard gasped as he stood up. He grinned at the flustered crane, whose face was covered in red bee stings.

"You are welcome." He bowed.

Festus squawked and crossed his wings.

"Now," Captain said grumpily. "What do we do about the fire?"

An hour later, as the moon was high in the sky, they set off again. The fire was extinguished and they were covered in soot.

None of them noticed the pack of coyotes leering in the woods behind them. They didn't notice the vulture perched high above them in the trees, watching their every move with beady eyes. They continued, shovels over their shoulders and lanterns swinging.

"I think we are almost there," the captain said excitedly.

The light danced frantically in the trees around them, agitated as they drew close to the place where the treasure lay.

Chapter Eight

When at last the crew came to a halt in a clearing, the light followed and, to their surprise, vanished into the ground.

"That's it," breathed the captain. Festus looked at him. "So we dig?" Floyd looked between them.

"Isn't something horrible supposed to happen now? This all seems too easy."

"Exactly what I was thinking," came the nefarious tone from the leader of the pack as the coyotes leaped into the clearing, surrounding the crew.

The crew drew close, back-to-back, facing the coyotes, shovels brandished threateningly. Rex snapped at them, stopping in front of the captain.

"Not quite so brave without your possum." Rex delicately held his Colt .38 super in a sleek paw, trained directly on the captain.

The other coyotes pulled their revolvers from inside their crisp, spotless jackets and vests. The captain's hand hovered over his hip, where he had slung a sawed-off shotgun.

"Ah, ah, ah… old friend," Rex sneered. "You won't be needing that."

He gestured with his free paw, and the crew was quickly overtaken and stripped of their weapons. They were bound tightly together with strong rope. The coyotes circled the helpless crew, pacing while awaiting the command from their leader to attack. Rex grinned, his teeth gleaming in the moonlight.

"How does it feel? To lose everything?" He chuckled.

There was a sound of flapping wings as the vulture appeared

in the clearing, settling onto the stark branch of a dead tree.

"Good work, Rex, my friend," he rasped, shifting back and forth on his perch. "Captain." He sighed. "It seems that you have left me no choice." His beady eyes narrowed. "After all the time I have given you. After all the favors you have asked of me! And you treat me so disrespectfully. You run from me. You lie to me." He gestured with a wing to the pack. "You threaten my men." Shaking his head, he snapped his beak together. "You leave me no choice, Captain."

The vulture squawked out orders to the pack to begin digging where the crew had begun.

"You have proved useful to me in that you have led me to the treasure." He turned back to the captain. "So I will spare your life. But your boat…" He shrugged his wings. "It will be mine. And your crew, they are of no use to me." With a menacing nod, he looked to Rex. "Kill the crew."

The captain roared and strained against his ropes as he was dragged away from the crew. Rex picked up the captain's shotgun from the pile on the ground.

"This seems perfect for the job." He flashed a grin at the captain.

"Stop this! Stop!" Captain barked at the vulture. "I will do anything you ask.

Anything!" he whined, his tone pathetic.

The vulture cackled.

"Captain, Captain. How would you learn your lesson? You have nothing I want. You are useless to me now."

He motioned to Rex to continue. The captain roared and growled, but Rex stepped toward the crew.

A terrific howl broke out in the clearing, and they turned to the sound. The ground tore as if rent apart by the hands of God, and from the crevice, rising from the ground in the

place where the treasure was, came a glowing blue light.

The light took shape of a massive skeletal bear, his fur matted and his claws long and sharp. His eyes were blinding blue lights, lighting up the clearing.

The coyotes shrank back from the light, whimpering. The bear was ten feet tall. When he tilted back his head and opened his mouth, from behind his razor-sharp teeth came a roar that shook the ground. The coyotes trembled in their places, and the crew shuddered in their bindings.

"The Fifolet," squeaked the vulture. "The legends are true!"

"Do something!" he screeched to the coyotes. The coyotes, quaking with fear, did no such thing. Frozen to the ground, they were unable to move as the bear surged toward them with the grace of a shadow.

As the blue light passed through the pack, slashing at the coyotes with long claws, there were flashes of blinding light as each coyote was hit, and they vanished into the air.

The vulture, realizing that his protection was gone, took flight and soared over the scene. Just as his wings crested the tops of the trees, the bear floated toward him, and with one outstretched paw, struck him from the air.

With a horrific sound, the vulture vanished. Rex, trembling, his paws tight around the stock, let loose a spray of bullets, firing the shotgun rapidly into the shape of the bear. This served only as a nuisance, and when the shot passed through the shadow, not affecting it, Rex dropped the shotgun, turned around and attempted to flee. He was caught and disappeared.

All that was left in the clearing was the crew, and the scattered shovels.

The bear turned to where the crew were tied to the tree and let out a terrific growl that shook the earth. He lumbered slowly toward them. His teeth gleamed in the moonlight.

Chapter Nine

The crew shook with fear as the bear approached. It lumbered forward, slobber dripping over razor-sharp teeth. His claws dug into the soft mud as he walked. The crew fought with all their might against their bindings, but the ropes held tight.

Captain snapped and growled at the bear, his hackles raised as it approached. He fought like a rabid dog, his teeth snapping.

"HEY!" A sudden shout rang through the clearing.

The bear turned with a snarl to face the newcomer. There, in the midst of the clearing, stood Clovis. His fur was singed, he limped, and he was covered in mud and twigs, but he stood there, teeth bared.

"Come and get me, you big, rotting beast!" he growled at the Fifolet. The bear wheeled and charged toward the fox.

Clovis stood his ground, teeth bared and fur standing on end. "Clovis, no!" Captain shouted.

The bear swung a massive paw at Clovis, swiping at the fox like he was a gnat. Clovis leapt out the way, still snarling. He danced around the bear on light paws.

The bear roared and wheeled, swiping at the fox.

The crew shouted and fought against the ropes as Clovis continued to dance around the bear.

"Hey there, Murphy." Captain heard the purring voice in his ear.

"Marie!" Captain exclaimed, writhing against the ropes to see the cat standing behind them.

She held a knife in the air, the moonlight gleaming on the steel.

"I always have to get you out of these tough spots, beb," she gloated as she set to work sawing at the ropes.

The ropes let loose, freeing Murphy. Immediately, he ran to the crew and freed them. They turned to face the bear in time to see him take a swipe at Clovis. The bear's paw grazed the fox and sent him screaming as he flew through the air. He landed with a thud on the forest floor and lay still.

"Clovis, no!" Floyd yelled, rushing to his side. He moved slowly, and Abelard beat him there, dropping to the ground at the fox's side.

"Come on, you great beast!" Cap roared at the bear, bracing himself.

He grabbed a shovel off of the ground, the closest thing he could find, and brandished it in the air.

The bear pawed the ground and roared. Then, he charged. Captain raised the shovel above his head and howled, the loudest howl he could. Marie braced herself at his side, hissing. Her eyes blazed, and her fur stood on end.

The Fifolet slid to a stop in front of them, rearing up onto his hind legs and swiping at them. Captain swung the shovel, bringing it down on the bear's shoulder. The shovel whooshed through like it was made of air. The Fifolet caught the caption with his paw and sent him flying.

"Murphy!" Marie screamed, running to where he had landed on the ground.

Captain opened his eyes, gasping as he clutched at his chest where the gaping wound should be. Instead, he grasped the charm at the end of a chain. Marie slid on her knees in the dirt, falling to his side.

"The charm!" He gasped. "It worked! It saved me!"

"Oh, Murphy, you old fool!" she howled at him, throwing her arms around his neck.

The bear dropped to all fours and pawed the ground again, preparing for a charge. Marie braced herself, throwing her body over the captain's.

Suddenly, the bear reared up, roaring loudly. Flames crackled at his paws, licking his fur until it engulfed him. Then, with a final roar, he disappeared, only a heap of ash remaining.

"Wha-What?" Captain gasped, looking with disbelief at the place where the bear had been standing.

The crew gaped at the empty clearing, unsure what had just happened. A sudden scratching noise came from the hole where the treasure lay.

The crew backed away, scrambling to be as far as they could from whatever would emerge.

The scratching grew louder and more frantic until, suddenly, out from the hole leapt a small shape covered in mud.

"Ahhhh!" they screeched.

The shape jumped in the air, startled and grasping his whiskers. "Ahhh!" squeaked Marcel, shaking the mud from his fur.

"What are y'all screeching about?" He sniffed, cleaning his tail. "Didn't I just take care of the Fifolet?"

They stared at the ancient rat with disbelief.

"Nuh uh." Marie shook her head. "You did not just destroy a guardian spirit like it was nothing."

Marcel shrugged and hiccupped.

"Everyone knows, when you have a ghost, you burn the bones!" he squeaked, tossing a spent match over his shoulder.

The crew exchanged wide-eyed looks.

Clovis sat up from the ground with a groan, holding his shoulder. "What happened?" he barked. "Did I save the day?"

The crew exchanged looks once more. Then the clearing erupted in laughter. "Somebody grab a shovel!" Cap barked. "We have some treasure to dig up!"

Breathless and still shaking with adrenaline, the crew reached the water's edge and started up the ramp to the boat. Over their shoulders, they carried sacks of treasure.

The sound of a gun being cocked stopped them in their tracks. Into the lantern light that shone from the cabin stepped several small, gleaming martins, impeccably dressed. Their hats kept their faces in the shadows, yet their beady eyes gleamed in the lamplight.

"The family," gasped Abelard.

The captain stepped to stand in front of his crew.

"Silver Dollar Sam," he grunted. "What can I do for you?" Sylvester stood tall at the front of the group of martins.

"We are looking for the vulture." His silky voice floated through the night. "Well, he's gone," the captain said flatly. "Along with his pack."

The martin started visibly.

"Gone?" he snapped. "What do you mean?"

The captain shrugged. "Gone, dead, vanished. Just gone."

A vole scurried from the woods and, straightening his suit, whispered in Sylvester's ear.

"Signs of a struggle in the woods, boss. No signs of the vulture left. Whatever happened, they're gone for good."

Sylvester looked at the captain.

"Marie told us you were here. She told us about the Fifolet. I suppose you didn't believe her either." He smirked. "I guess we were both wrong."

Marie smirked. "They never listen to me, Sammy boy."

Sam gestured to his man, who lowered the gun he had trained on the crew.

"I owe you thanks, Captain. If only indirectly, you have done me a great service." He chuckled softly. "And however it was done, Provenzano is gone, and for that, I am in your debt."

He gestured to his men.

"Consider yourself a friend of the family, and under my protection." The captain nodded his thanks and respect.

"Keep your boat, Captain." Sylvester tapped the railing. "Consider the debt forgiven. The vulture's dealings mean nothing to me."

And then, as quickly as they had appeared, the martins left, shadows into the night.

Clovis hesitated a moment before saying, "They run a gambling operation don't they?"

Captain nodded.

"Well then, thanks for the getaway, old buddy, but I see a bright future that way." He pointed after the retreating family. "Shrimping really isn't my thing, you know."

After dashing down the stairs to don his old suit, he came back above deck, straightening the lapels. "Gentlemen," he sighed. "It has been my honor and privilege to take on this monstrous adventure with you all. If you are ever in the quarter, look me up!"

The captain put one paw on Clovis's shoulder and smiled. "You aren't half bad, fox," he said.

"Yeah," Festus said grudgingly. "I hate to say it, you sly beast, but you really came through for us. I'm sorry for calling you a coward."

Clovis shrugged and smirked. "Yeah, I'm not that bad once you get to know me." Captain stepped back, holding out a paw to the fox.

"You are always welcome on the Trouble II, Clovis," he said. "And you are always welcome in my crew."

Clovis nodded and smiled, wiping away a tear discreetly. Then, with a wave, he leaped down the ramp and bounded along the path after the martins.

The captain sighed, as did the crew. They were free once more. No ties, no debts, only the water and their trade. There was an air of total peace on board, and as they pulled up anchor and set course for open water, they were completely happy. The crickets sang their sweet song, and the birds whistled merrily as the sun began to rise over the bayou.

"Hey, boys, what do you think we ought to do with all this loot?" the captain called the crew, laughing.

The boat chugged merrily through the muddy water. The crew talked and laughed amongst themselves. None of them knew what adventure lay ahead, but they had each other. That, and a hold full of treasure, was enough.

CPSIA information can be obtained
at www.ICGtesting.com
Printed in the USA
BVHW090803140623
665881BV00016B/980